PARABLES OF ASSORTED FLAVOURS

OLUSOLA SOPHIA ANYANWU

With great gratitude to the lovely Holy Spirit
for His inspiration

WRITTEN FROM 2002 TO 2008

ISBN: 978-1-915398-42-0

www.olusolasophiaanyanwuauthor.com

Contents

This book is dedicated to to my daughters:
Chiamaka and Chiasoka

THE AFRICAN QUEEN AND HER NOBLE GUEST

CHAPTER 1

April 2003

THIS NOBLE GUEST has a secret. He often visits the Queen for spiritual matters and knows the palace area and surroundings like the palm of his hands. This excerpt is from his diary in which he describes the palace, leaving no doubt that the Queen is as complex and confusing as the description of her palace. He adds details of the palace based on his observations during each visit over a two-year period. He graciously declined hotel accommodation to the Queen's honourable request that he sojourn in her palace after his official tour of the local diocese in the area.

The Queen's Palace is situated on a mini hill and surrounded by walls. The palace is fronted by a giant iron gate providing for a car drive and a pedestrian entrance. The front drive is situated on a concrete floor that extends to the palace wall. On the left side of the palace wall is a garage for a car. On each side of the external wall, another concrete floor runs, approximately eight feet wide, from the gate to the back of the palace and extends to the Boys' Quarters behind the palace. The concreted floor on the right-hand side reaches to a car garage annexed to the Boys' Quarters.

Again, on each side of the concreted floor lies a garden extending to the wall fence of the palace. The gardens are filled with a variety of plants: flowers, vegetables, fruit trees, plantain, banana trees, maize plots, yam plots, and other edibles too numerous to mention. An upstairs veranda canopies the arrival port. A glazed iron door leads into a mini, narrow, stripped veranda on the right-hand side of which lies a toilet. There is yet another iron door that leads into the Queen's living room. Suffice it to say that the living room is royalty defined!

It was the 9th of April 2003, when the eminent noble guest alighted from his Mercedes-Benz 200 car at the front of the Iron Gate and walked into the palace premises through the pedestrian gate. The Queen, who was already expecting her guest, suddenly emerged from somewhere in the vicinity of the premises. She met her guest at the entrance to the palace. She swung her sumptuous body into a delectable hug of her guest, who was hardly expecting so much warmth for a welcome. Her body was decorated and arrayed in a plain, pinkish dress, and she gallantly led her guest into the Royal palace, sitting him on a carefully selected, comfortable seat in the living room. There was television to watch and a variety of music to enjoy, but none of this came to play at this moment.

The Queen, herself, sat at a hearing distance from her noble guest, who was richly attired and in a position remote enough to keep the guest well apart. Drinks and light refreshment began to pour in for the guest, while lively discussions were going on between the two. Most of the discussion consisted of reminiscences of the past, as both the queen and the guest were former colleagues for many years at the bar before he entered the ministry of the Lord God of Hosts. The rest of the day was spent talking, eating and drinking. The closest the guest was allowed to approach the queen was an invitation from the queen for the guest to inspect a dark spot on the left shoulder of the queen.

With the Queen's permission and direction, the guest, with his index finger, touched the dark dot. Even though the guest would have loved not only to feel the dark dot but also to stroke the soft velvet-like skin holding the dot, he dared not lest the fury of the queen be aroused and his secret be exposed! Earlier, the hostess had shown her guest round the house to the top part of the building and the veranda, which he had never visited. He nearly struggled to keep his control. The Queen's bedroom was firmly locked, he had noticed. The guest felt the electrified air blazing around them from the heat of chemistry between them!

At dusk, the guest was shown to the Guest room on the ground floor. It was a comfortable enough place. In a bid to provide adequate comfort to her guest, Her Royal Highness personally entered the Guest room with the

Guest to ensure that the soap, towels, and other necessities for the Guest in the bathroom, annexed to the Guest room, were available and in good order. In doing so, she entered her guest's bedroom in a frail manner, watching diligently like a timid mouse afraid to pass by a cat lest it be caught by the eager, hungry cat. The Guest honourably kept his distance till Her Royal Majesty swung out of the room. A young, pretty teenage girl named Mimi was asked to tidy the bathroom for the guests' early morning wash-up.

After a lavish dinner with the Queen that first day, she and her Guest decided to have an evening lazing out on the concrete floor in front of the palace. They sat cosily and reminisced about many things until late at night. Mosquitoes began to whirl around their feet, and the Guest made a motion to postpone the rest of their tete-a-tete till the next day. He stood up and offered to give a goodnight kiss to Her Royal Majesty. In a swift reaction to the offer, Her Royal Highness immediately sprang up from her seat and took to her heels to avoid the brazen bid by her noble Guest. Undaunted and in a bid to ward off the shame of the rebuff, the Guest raced to catch up with the Queen and was able to overtake her at the entrance of the palace's living room. This attempt too was rebuffed with, "I am not your wife", spoken with shut eyes that closed out effectively whatever emotions the Queen had for her noble Guest. She slithered away. Overcome with overwhelming shame, the Guest held his peace and walked into his lonely guestroom downstairs, carrying raw, painful feelings of disappointment and disgrace.

CHAPTER 2

THE NEXT MORNING, the Guest left the palace unceremoniously with his driver to purchase fuel for his car. The watchful Queen wondered whether the noble Guest had surreptitiously taken a French leave and departed. However, the Guest later returned with his driver, and the Queen did not mince words, expressing her surprise and wondering if the Guest had indeed departed. Such an unceremonious departure would have been derogation from the Guest's nobility…

Upstairs, where Her Royal Majesty slept, she tidied up and got well dressed. She descended the stairs to meet her Guest, who was already sitting waiting for Her Royal Highness to show up. To the Guest's great amazement and amusement, the hostess went down on her knees to greet her guest 'Good Morning, Sir.' The noble guest's normal reaction to such staggering courtesy was to quickly move to Her Royal Majesty, hold her by the two hands and gracefully lift her. He, however, restrained himself lest such a gesture lead to a negative reaction from the Queen…

The noble Guest was to depart the palace early on the third day. He woke up early and got himself ready for departure. Emerging from his lonely room, he saw the

Queen standing in the kitchen of the palace with her back turned to the dining apartment, apparently getting breakfast ready. The noble Guest blurted out, "My special cook". Without uttering a word, Her Royal Majesty suddenly turned, facing the noble Guest and suddenly hugged him! The Guest was incredibly delighted by this affectionate hug. He felt like reciprocating this gesture by fiddling with his hands on the Queen's back and sides, but he instead stood speechless and motionless like a statue while enjoying the surprising gesture by the Queen. Later, the Queen treated her Guest to a luscious breakfast, joining him at the table with lively discussions. It was a send-off breakfast. Earlier, the Queen had dispatched her driver and Mimi to the market to purchase lovely gifts for the Guest. When they arrived, they loaded the Guest's car with lots of gift wines, yams, fresh maize, plantains and a live fowl. Her Royal Majesty stood at the lobby of the palace with Tomi, her grandson and Mimi to say farewell to her guest.

The Queen was impeccably well-dressed, and her perfume added a sweet note to the atmosphere. She looked radiant and attractive. At the painful departure, the noble Guest wished so badly that he could give the Queen a final hug and pecks on the rosy cheeks of her fair-skinned face, but he painfully restrained himself. He took a final wistful look at her full bosom, her rounded hips and slim waistline without being obvious. He knew he could not afford to end up despicable in her thoughts. So, he merely entered his car, waving Her Royal Majesty and her household goodbye!

FAMILY AND HOME

Room

Sharon's favourite room is situated in 46 Coral Walk in Dartford, Kent. It is her mistress's daughter's room, and surprisingly, not hers! It is a large room where, at any time of day, you will find clothes scattered on the carpet, bed, table, bookshelf, and some spilling out of the closets. The room has a murky smell of indescribable odours, including stale food left on a plate for over three days, and an overflowing bin containing a range of discarded items, from clothing and objects to food, stationery, and soiled sanitary pads. The walls are full of holes from the puncture of nails. A few eye-catching photographs depict her mistresses' daughters at an early age, below ten, displayed alongside other hero worship pictures. There is significant evidence that the walls suffer from dampness, drought, and wetness due to weather conditions and occasional bedsheet accidents. Of course, all these blend into the murky smell of the room.

Apart from unwashed plates, cups, and cutlery, there is a large laundry basket that has crumpled under the weight of dirty clothes flung haphazardly from all angles of the room. The majority of the flung clothing [pants, bras, socks, etc] did not meet the target and are left strewn all over the room.

Several cupboards cannot be strictly classified as bookshelves, as they contain clothes, objects, and hair accessories, among other items. The makeup cupboard has a top that resembles a hybrid between a pantry and a makeup table, as drinks and food items have been left to share space with the makeup.

The radiator in the room has been converted into a towel rack. Wet towels have been dumped on it along with wet shower caps. This makes very befitting ugly patches on the walls. Some other towels have been left on the bed.

The beds are never or rarely laid, except by Sharon's hands. The beds, as if served for breakfast, have a mix of sleeping clothes, a bag from an overturned hair accessories kit, books, food, and the beddings can be sworn in as the most wanted by the washing machine!

Sharon has to pick her way nimbly as she enters this room, and there are a lot of things on the ground which are vying for the attention of Sharon's feet to trip her as if in a dribbling ball game. Things like shoes, clothes, hangers, stationery, a brush, lots of hair strands and bags!

Sharon always imagines that if any family member were looking for a specific item in this room, they would give up on it. All missing items of any member of 43 Coral Walk decides best to wait until Sharon has finished her work on Fridays. Sharon finds stuff in every part of this room. Sometimes, missing items can be found under the beds, which remains another secret adventure.

Indeed, these daughters have survived in this room for eight years, since Sharon got the contract in 2004. In August 2012, these girls were converted to ladies by rescuing them from their jungle and relocating them to different venues of abode.

Sharon will never forget her favourite room, how she used to smile each Friday as she stepped into this haven of paradise. It was her ticket to life for herself and her only son. She had set her foot in during school time from 9 am, and by 12 noon, she was done. On school vacations, her timetable shift was flexible. She would await a call from her mistress with eagerness. She never had the chance to meet these daughters in person, but she knew their names, their schools, their ages, and everything else imaginable about them. Will they ever appreciate the labour of love the twenty-eight-year-old Polish lady served to them when they lived like animals?

Sharon will never forget her favourite room!

EXPERIENCE

Amazing Job

THE YOUNG MAN applied for a job somewhere in London in 2012. He was pretty lucky to be called for an interview. During the interview, the twenty-two-year-old brought out a sheet of paper on which he had carefully and thoughtfully written some expected questions and their answers. He kept referring to this paper when asked questions. It reached a point where the interviewer covered up the man's paper with questions and answers, which was open in front of him on the table.

Miraculously, the young adult got the job. For one month, he laboured. He worked. He sweated. He sacrificed weekends. He rose early each morning from South East London to North London and came home late at night. It was August, when the weather is hot, unbearable, but cool at night. Then all of a sudden, the job ends. He wasn't needed any more.

Several months later, he has not been paid!!!

EXPECTATION

Car Wash

Augustus had his car washed at the car wash near Lidl in 2007. He came home with a shiny car, and, in addition, as if it were a trophy, he received an air freshener in the bargain. As he told his family this unbelievable tale, his father naturally became interested. Off he went to the carwash. He bargained with the car wash boys and got a fair price for the car wash, which was much cheaper than his sons'.

He watched as the car wash boys did their job, at the same time feeling great and pleased with the price he had bargained for. At the finish point, he collected the car and gave the money to the car wash boys, saying, 'Thank you', and added, 'Where is the air freshener?'

'Not at the price you have paid for, Sir!!'

GRATITUDE

Towel

THE YEAR WAS 2004. Chima was a few weeks old in the UK and in need of a quality towel from the UK as he had discarded his hardy, thick towel from Nigeria. His wife naturally got him one that same week – but he was full of complaints:

'Why, this towel is even worse than my towel from Nigeria!

'This towel does not absorb the water on my body!'

'I can't stand this towel. It feels coarse...' On and on went the complaints, so his wife decided that he could get one for himself from the shops, and so, he bought a new towel. The next morning, being a Saturday, the new towel was launched. Chima used his new, big white towel. Then he came into the room and his wife split from laughing off her sides. On his hair, eyebrows, eyelids, and skin on the face were all sprinkled with white droppings from the towel. Then he looked in the mirror and could not believe his eyes. Indeed, he looked as if he had been covered in white powder all over his head and face! Eventually, of course, the towel was never used again. It was demoted. It was used as a spread cloth on the ironing table. As time went on, it became too old and unsightly to continue serving as an ironing table cover, and it became a rag in the kitchen for mopping floors and cleaning up spills on the carpet in the living room.

Now, Chima uses the towel his wife bought for him initially.

VULNERABILITY

MOTHERHOOD

I HAD MY first baby on September 19, 1983, and my last on October 7, 1997. Between those years till date, I have mothered, nursed, nurtured, defended, played God and anything else you can imagine. Of course, I also backed, carried, entertained, and taught these children.

I recently acquired another 'baby' by accident – November 2012. He was already a grown man of 62 but needed to be bathed, toileted, dressed, put to bed, given his drugs, nursed, calmed, soothed, nourished... following a delicate surgery!

Motherhood is an acquired skill. It is inborn, natural, tender, instinctive, knowledge, wisdom, a talent that gets tender with the years.

OFFSPRING

SOME MOTHERS DO HAVE THEM!

I AM IN the group of the 'Some'...

Is it good to have them? Is it wonderful to have them? Do I feel great and on top of the world to have them? I wish I could answer these questions without leaving a doubt in your mind. Anyway, have a go at what you are going to read and make your own judgement - but don't forget to thank God!!

There is something special about being the lastborn – I mean, those children called 'baby of the family,' 'the youngest child,' or 'the last child,' etc. In September 2016, three weeks before my last child left for uni, I started feeling nostalgia. I found myself becoming emotional. Perhaps this was partly responsible for categorising me with 'those mothers who do have them'. I found myself doing all her laundry. I became her feet and went to her room, tidied it up and got all the dirty clothing out, unwashed plates, unwanted bedlinens, over full bins, etc all sorted out.

I became her hands. I got out the boxes for uni, packed up all the uni shopping, and arranged them, ensuring that bedding, stationery, underwear, clothing, provisions, etc. were all packed in.

I also became her brain. I asked her to take a bath, wash her hair, eat, get her hair done, and think about what other clothes she wanted packed into her box or did not want. I helped her ensure that she had cooked food to take to uni for her fridge. We took her to uni on 17/09/2016. I continued to be her hands, feet, and brain as I helped her unpack the boxes, sort the clothes into the cupboard, foodstuffs into the kitchen, and various accessories into different compartments.

Finally, I made her bed and placed the suitcases on top of the wardrobe. I did this after I had ensured her toilet bag was ready, slippers out, and bathrobe hung on a hook, and… Finally, finally, I left my lastborn at 4 pm to start fending for herself!

DAUGHTERS

PRINCESS

SHE IS MY fourth child and first daughter. This evening, at
9 pm, precisely, marked the 21st of September 2016. She
came into my room to show me the wedding pics of a
wedding belonging to her friend's mum. Many things
occurred to me at once. How regal! How royal! How lovely!
What a privilege! What a rare surprise! How advantageous!
How befitting! How truly warm and cosy for mother and
daughter in the space of one hour to travel down memory
lane of the yesteryears and orbit the fringes of the future!!
How amazing to get close to the heart of my princess that
had been – what can I say – the sole benefit of her bosom
friends: Debby, Naddy, Gracey, Kemmy, Toyssy, etc. She is
a very social being who enjoys social gatherings and gracing
social events and wants to be a 'Londonite'.

Well, sharing her hopes, aspirations, her loves, her
future plans and so on drew her close to my heart. I realised
how beautiful, mature, grown-up and thoughtful the
princess is!!

In one hour, we both realised how free it was to talk and chat with ease about anything. The best bit of it all is that the princess loves her family and home. She wants to live at home and work nearby. You see!! Surprising!! Princess is special… Home is too!!

...A GOOD THING

Goodbye Darling

My husband and I were both expecting Soka, our youngest, to come home for the weekend. Her birthday was on Friday, 7th October, so we expected her to come home late on Friday evening or Saturday morning. We got the distressed call that her trip was cancelled. How shocking!! Considering that we had heard her tales of woe, including hunger, shortages of food, and missing home-cooked meals. On the spur of the moment, I decided to take the trip to visit her in Birmingham on 8th October, 2016.

Straightaway, my husband quickly took it upon himself and, of utmost urgency, got my online ticket all sorted out. In no little time, two tickets were printed out for me, and a stage-by-stage self-handwritten journey planner was written out for me on plain white paper. It consisted of detailed information on how and when I would depart:

Depart from Bexleyheath Station at 9 am. Arrive at London Victoria Station at 10.30 am. Get to London

Victoria Coach Station to get the 11.30 coach to Birmingham. Arrive at Birmingham at 2 pm. Get a taxi to Soka's address.

On another separate paper, Soka's address was written. It was a small piece of paper to fit into my purse. 'Show this to the driver,' he said. 'On another larger paper, the same address was written. 'Just in case, the other address gets missing.'

Saturday, 8th October, arrived. Before we left the house, we had prayed, and I had told him to take good care of himself while I was gone. We left home by 8.20 am for Bexleyheath Station. I was further armed with a 'return planner'. When we got there, he gave me further advice: 'Do not get into the wrong train.' After a moment's pause, 'Use the lift. It is over there after the steps.' Seconds later, I heard him say, 'I'm concerned about all those papers. Do not let your ticket and the address fall out of your purse.' To all this, I was calm, relaxed, and confident that all his good advice was falling on open ears. So, I replied, 'Everything is ok, darling.'

We said our goodbyes. I said,' Bye darling' and he replied, 'Hmn hmn, ok take care,' and he drove off. He isn't sentimental with endearments!

LUGGAGE

Soka's Food

ALL THE WAY from Abbey Wood, South East London, to Birmingham, the following things were lugged through by train and coach for our last born on 8th October 2016:

* 2 bags of boiled chicken - 30 pieces
* 8 takeaway packs of stew
* £2 plantain [6 fingers]
* Burger bread
* Sausage rolls bread
* Garri powder
* Iyan powder
* 8 eggs
* A loaf of bread
* A jar of white pepper
* Onga spices - 20 sachets
* 2 large packs of Jollof rice

* 1 pack of chicken curry
* 6 packets of Chinchin
* 1 nylon of groundnut
* 2 warm tops
* 1 blanket
* An old lab coat
* 1 black polo neck blouse
* 1 packet of burger grill
* 1 packet of frankfurter
* 2 boxes of lasagne for the oven

BIRTHDAY

OCTOBER 9 2016

THIS DAY MET me at Birmingham. It was the most unique birthday I've ever had. I was far away from receiving calls from our landline or my mobile phone. My phone was dead. Duchess had ordered a new phone for herself, but had none. And so in quiet and peace, mother and daughter arranged the house to look cleaner and tidier. Later, Duchess did her laundry, and I helped her. We had lunch – she ate rice and curry, while I ate bread, eggs, and frankfurters. Duchess had some fried eggs and frankfurter too. After this, we listened to Joel Osteen, discussed her university stuff, friends, lecturers, transport, holidays, money, and everything else not mentioned. I learned that her friend, Jummy, gave her a lovely cash gift!! Wow.

Soon it was bedtime. And that was the end of October 9th.

HABIT

Transition?

Grandma has lived in the new home of Frank and Alice, along with their latest addition, her newest grandchild, for two weeks. Praise God. This new home shows a very high quality of taste in colours, textures, fittings and house stuff. Also, there is a very high level of cleanliness, almost humanly impossible to attain, without God's grace. She doesn't really think it is because the man and wife are both doctors – No. It is a complex combination of various issues. The kitchen and dining area are spotless. When she drops a piece of cloth, a speck, or tissue, it is glaringly apparent. When she washes up in the sink, it must be left as if no one used it. The kind of way professional cleaners in the UK clean up kitchens or toilets. Even after bathing, there should be no memory of recent usage. Caution, precaution, carefulness, extra care and being utterly careful is the lifestyle in this lovely house at 29 Courageous Way, Chelsea. You really have to endeavour and be courageous to visit or stay.

After Grandma's first night, her daughter Alice did up her room. She got the hint: Lay up your bed with style and puff up the pillows. After she had used the kitchen sink, it was reworked again and again. She got the message: dry up the sink, leave things to dry on the rack, clean up all surfaces, and mop the floor, if you please! Each time Grandma used the loo, she left the lid down. Soon, she realised the opposite each time she revisited the loo. Grandma got the message: 'Do in Rome as the Romans do' OR 'when you get to your own castle, you can rule your toilet, kitchen and bathroom as you like'. So, Grandma always left the loo seat up – as most husbands prefer. And around the house? Grandma got the facts straight. A 'ssh' when she's calling out on the stairs or a warning [polite] – 'Mum, please lower your voice.'

Grandma has now become a bona fide, certified, full-fledged member of the house in maintaining very high-quality hygiene and cleanliness. So transformed is she that on getting back to her castle, it is stifling, unbearable and almost uninhabitable. She straight away tries to enforce the same standards of hygiene and cleanliness. So transformed is she that her two sons, Chimy and Chisy, think she is in the wrong house or talking Greek. They think their mum has gone nuts. They cannot imagine or phantom what she has seen, done, and experienced. It's beyond their imagination. They beg her to 'take it easy'.

The transition was something else, as Grandma flashes back her memory: As she walked through the door into her residence, bits of debris and litter welcomed her. She goes straight to the downstairs loo, uses it, and throws the lid up. Behold! She understood perfectly why it is best to leave the seat up in a man's world fashion. When she entered the kitchen, Chimy was sitting comfortably in the area, a major stakeholder in the contribution of what she had seen.

The door of the fridge was soiled red. The refrigerator has not had a bath for over 5 weeks!! The floor was littered. There were baskets of unwashed laundry. The kitchen bin was waiting for attention... The sink area was piled to overflowing to the point of alarm! The surface area of the cooker showed signs of previous activities, including frying, mixing, drinking, and cooking.

Grandma goes to the living room area and realises that someone has indeed cleaned and vacuumed the carpet but did not do a thorough job of dusting the centre table. She climbs up to the bedroom area, and the horrors there she beholds throw her down to helplessness and defeat. Chimy and Chisy's rooms have been turned upside down by a kind of invisible avalanche passing through. The bathroom is filthy – the scums on the bathtub defy the cleansing agent. The sink, the floor, the curtains, the toilet, all welcome her back, not for their salvation but back to her world!!

She has a battle plan…

CHEF

Daddy's Special

On 2nd April 2017, 'Daddy's Special' was prepared. As part of our trip to visit our younger daughter, Duchess, at University far, far away in Birmingham, my husband agreed to organise what the family calls 'Daddy's Special'. It is a meal of Jollof spaghetti with the renowned meatballs and vegetables in it. On my part, I advised our buying Tasty Jollof rice to save us the stress of cooking: get a big, clean pot out, grind the ingredients, boil the meat, slice the onions, wash up, etc. My husband insisted that he would still go ahead and prepare the 'Daddy's Special'.

On the eve of Monday, which was Sunday, we went to church, visited our 'famous' Chinese restaurant in Dartford and returned home with over-gorged stomachs. Sleep was my next agenda. When I woke up, the next agenda was to sit in the living room, watch TV in peace and harmony, and go through my phone and emails. It was a delightful atmosphere, mood and evening. It felt like 'Mummy

Special'. I had previously cooked Jollof rice for the week and had no business with the kitchen.

Suddenly, my lovely world was about to rock when my husband said, or rather commanded, 'Go and bring the big pot out.' I got up to obey, but gave a polite, gentle reminder that it was his last command to me as regards the preparation of 'Daddy's Special'. We both left for the kitchen. I brought out the big pot and returned to the living room to enjoy the sole monopoly of the remote, TV, the settee and indeed the entire living room. When my conscience gnawed at me after an interval of two good, whole hours, the good Lord told me to enjoy 'Mummy Special' as my darling husband was engaging in his 'Daddy Special'.

So, I sat back and continued enjoying the moment...

ACCLIMATISATION

Suffer Head

Suffer head? This refers to people who are accustomed to hardship or people who have endured lack and adverse conditions without their realising it. This is because they sail through life padded all around with God's grace. Chima and I were travelling. We did not live very far away from the nearest bus stop, which was about a three-minute walk from the house. Instead, on this sunny day, Chima lugged on a hand luggage which had 30 cups of rice, onions, tin tomatoes, uni textbooks, 40 packets of Indomie and one or two packets of spaghetti and started to trudge determinedly, slow but challenging, the 15 minutes' walk or more to the train station! And in my own hand luggage, I had also packed 15 takeaway packs of frozen Jollof rice, two large packs of frozen 'Daddy Special', 1 bag of frozen boiled chicken, 1 bag of frozen fried chicken, and one large bucket of All-purpose seasoning. All these were for our daughter at the University of Birmingham, whom we were visiting, that cold autumn of 2018.

The weight was unbelievable. I had my handbag and sweater on one arm and trudged decidedly but slowly and painfully after my husband. After a while, a bus passed by us, and I asked my husband a simple question, 'What harm would it have cost us if we had taken a bus to the train station?'

CAREER

Duchess

THE DUCHESS OF Akpim is the younger daughter of the Duchess of Thamesmead.

In May 2017, it was announced that a certain duchess was taking a drastic step akin to jumping off from a high cliff! This duchess made a U–turn from the norm of both the Sunshine and the Crown tradition values. What did she do? She said she was going to make a hobby, a lifetime career!!! Was she serious? Well, she told the entire family that she was going to pull out of uni!! Everyone thought it was a joke until she made it clear that it was not a joke. To save the situation, numerous prayers, fasts, and advice were offered through WhatsApp messages and verbal messages from other family members in earnest.

The question is – which rational-minded thinking female of the 21st-century generation will deem it possible even to give a thought that 'university education is not compulsory?' Considering our family background, that thought was 'living in a stone age mentality'. Well, all this really happened. A lot of thought processes and explanations by way of suggestions, reasons, views, and motives were ushered for the action of this duchess: Academic laziness? University life boredom? Not going to church? Straying away from God? Effects of modern technology? Following poor role models as friends? Challenging course? The lastborn syndrome? Etc

I am glad to say that the idea to drop out of uni was timely aborted by God's divine intervention!

HOLIDAY

Dubai Holiday July 2017

My husband and I received the good news of a trip to Dubai to achieve two purposes:
- To see our new grandson and
- A holiday!!

The couple had recently moved into Dubai from Abu Dhabi, following a grand new and exciting job offer for our son. Excitedly, seeing that our son was in a generous mood, my husband asked him a question that had been bothering him for over seven months. So, still on the phone, my husband said, 'Son, hope all is well. I noticed that you've stopped paying that allowance you give me monthly for the past two months.'

Our son answered very cheerfully, saying that all was okay. In addition, he said that he had stopped the monthly allowance to enable him to pay for our tickets to Dubai! That is robbing Peter to pay Paul, my husband said to me in the midst of chuckling.

'Typical Ibo man,' I said mirthlessly.

HEALTH

THURSDAY NOVEMBER 8TH 2012

CHIMA AND I took a train, as if we were going on a picnic. He had a bag packed with overnight wear and stuff. We arrived at Guy's Hospital, went through all the routine tests, form-filling, and so on. Chima was calm, brave and outwardly relaxed. We talked of everything else except his deep-borne, naked fear of the pending major surgery. At 11:30 a.m., Chima went into the theatre, and I didn't get to see him until 7:30 p.m.

He looked very fair, fresh and 30 years younger. I marvelled...

FAMILY

Family Reunion 2017

There couldn't have been a better opportunity and time for this to have happened on Father's Day, June 19th, 2017. From Thamesmead, we have four members: my husband, myself, Princess, and Duchess. From Colchester, there are three members: Emmy, Onny, and Eberechi. From Dubai, there are four members: Tom, Dozzy, Blessing, and Asher. And from Northfleet, two members: Femi and Ayo.

We all met at Morgan's to have lunch, roast–style, reminiscent of a Christmas dinner! We bless God. We convened later at Mangold for pics and family bonding!

AUTHORITY

PHOTOGRAPH 2017

ON THE DAY of our departure from Dubai to the UK, it was August 16th. It was also our son Tom's birthday. We were scheduled to travel at night. I began the day with my usual routine of bathing, feeding and babysitting the children. By noon, it was nap time for baby Asher and rest time for me. My husband suddenly had a brain wave: 'Dress Asher in church clothes. I am going to dress fancy for a photograph.' I looked at the sleepy baby. He was the kind of person for whom sleep did not always come naturally. Lots of cooing, rocking, singing and the rest were involved. I had just achieved this and undressing him for a pic with his grandad was a very wrong move. I watched my husband go up to change. He had made it clear to me that he thought it was a good move. I could not argue or disobey my husband as he would take it as a slight to his male ego. So, I managed to wear another knicker for the baby and lo and behold, my husband came down to the living room looking regal in his sparkling white lace outfit.

Next, he needed a photographer. This happened to be the Duchess, who was most of the time in the wrong mood due to her headaches.

My husband carried the sleeping baby very carefully and was not pleased that the baby was not also dressed in fancy clothes. He chose the spot for the pic while the photographer had better options but my husband's authority prevailed.

At last, the pics were ready to be seen. There were four in all.

- PIC 1 – was too dark
- PIC 2 – had a background of the cartoon showing on TV!!
- PIC 3 – showed his eyes looking closed!!
- PIC 4 – showed my husband looking angry!!

He lashed out at the photographer – 'Why did you take these pics? Can't you take photographs? Why didn't you tell me that the background was not good? Why didn't you retake the dark pictures and the closed-eyed ones?' My husband fumed and could not be pacified until 3 hours later. I watched him, defeated, go back upstairs, climbing those flights of stairs to take off the white sparkling clothes.

Baby Asher was sleeping peacefully…

LOVE

ANOTHER BIRTHDAY – OCTOBER 9 2017

YAAY! I happen to turn 59 years young – Amazing how time flies. I was a merry grandmother who had three grandchildren and more on the way. I received gifts on this day worth mentioning. On Sunday, I received a lovely, worded birthday card and a large storybook from my Colchester family. The Northfleet Family and Duchess sent a review of my first book – 'Stories for younger generations'.

Princess gave me a perfume. Taylay, Onny's sister, gave me a lovely towel [except it was too blue]. My sister, Folly, promised me something later on. My Dubai family, extended family, friends and our church members sent well wishes.

My HUSBAND gave me the big, beautiful, promising towel he had intended for himself, but for the first time in our marriage, there was no card! It was his love that mattered to me that spoke louder than words on a card…

DECLUTTER

Hanger

On July 30, 2021, I took a bold step to organise my clothes wardrobe. I got rid of the old clothes and hung out my clothes neatly in the cupboard with hangers. As I picked up a hanger to hang a blouse, it triggered a memory in my husband's brain as he watched me. Then, speaking to me, he told me this tale:

'The other day, I took our clothes to the dry cleaners and carried a lot of our spare hangers. I told them, "I have brought you so many spare hangers so that you can give me a discount." He told me how expectant he had felt. The guy had said, "No, we don't need the hangers. There is more if you want!" My husband said he did not need them, and if they wanted to throw them away, they could. He left the place with some people's eyes glued in his direction...

He said he had felt sooo embarrassed!

PROPHET

New Arrival 18/07/2017

You know how it seems when you watch movies or read novels and hear stories directly or indirectly about the things that can happen or have really happened to people. Other people's experiences might be make no meaning until we ourselves are in their shoes.

When an experience of life happens to you, you begin to think about how those others had felt through that same experience. How did Lord Jesus put it? A prophet is not honoured in his own home!

My writing career kicked off in reality on the 18th of July 2017. When we returned home from Princess's graduation in Loughborough University, I got home to see my manuscript turned into a book! Granted it was getting to 12 midnight and we had had a long day right from 5am. We had travelled by coach and train. There had been lots of ceremonies, speech making, photograph taking, walking up and down from hall to hall and no major meal eaten throughout. A lot of money had been spent from lean pockets as well!

I brought my climax at the wrong time – 'Everybody, my book has arrived!'

Even I knew that the timing and moment for that announcement was off! Yet, I could not believe that my dear manuscript was now a book, and I was a writer! I AM A WRITER...

Nobody rushed out to see the book. Nobody held the book. I heard some tired voices mumble something like:

'Oh mum, that's good.'

'Ennnn, it has come.'

'Really, Mum?'

I will not bother to mention which remark was my husband's, Amy's or Soka's because one thing was constant – no enthusiasm and a complete lack of interest at the new arrival!

Today is the third day. No one even remembers the book came.

I became the unhonoured prophet.

Lord Jesus is always right!

LIFE

SOME THOUGHTFUL FACTS OF LIFE!

1. Children will grow up and leave the home.

2. People grow older.

3. Ageing definitely takes place as soon as you hit the button for 40.

4. Sex is not the same in a man or woman aged 50+

5. Thoughts of death start creeping into your thoughts as soon as you are 50+

6. Your son will definitely enjoy his wife's cooking better than yours [debatable].

7. As soon as your daughter crosses age 21, you start to hope a husband is waiting on the horizon.

8. At some point in your marriage journey, you wonder if you would have been happier somewhere else and with someone else [debatable].

9. At 60, you cannot regain or attain the weight you had when you were 50.

10. At 50+, some accessories adorn your dressing – eyeglasses, hearing aids, wigs, false teeth, and a walking stick [depending on what season of life you are journeying through.]

11. At 60, you become conscious of those who are already 70. It's only a decade away! Spouses do not remain married all their lives. Death will separate them.

ANGELS

ANSWERED PRAYERS

• On Monday, October 23, 2017, my darling husband took the trip all the way to the University of Birmingham to give the Duchess =Jollof rice, Daddy Special[spaghetti]chicken, turkey, meat, moinmoin, bread, butter, small sauce, my birthday gift to her and some spice. It was an unexpected windfall, and a dream come true!

• On Soka's coming back from uni for Xmas – December 2016, she had this huge, heavy suitcase. Right from Birmingham Station all the way to Abbey Wood Station, a stranger helped her carry her suitcase all the way!

• I was on my way to school, which is usually a twenty-minute walk from my home. It was a cold, snowy November, and the roads were treacherous. Despite my being careful, I slipped, fell and began to trudge slowly. I raised a prayer and barely three minutes later, Angel Charles appeared and drove me to school!

• My daughter was heavily pregnant but not yet quite due. A stranger observed that she attacked the itches on her body with aggression. The stranger urged her to get to the hospital without delay. She would have lost Baby Blessing if she had ignored the angel!

• The man of faith had done the driving test 3 times. Yet, he fasted, prayed and practised so hard. Surely this 4th time! The driving had not been error-free. After another mistake, he began to sweat, expecting to hear the worst. The Angel turned to him and said,' YOU PASSED'!

• Princess went for an interview at a very prestigious bank in London. Her vigorous preparation didn't arm her with confidence. The interviewer chatted informally with her about hobbies, food and movies. After some shared laughter, she was given the job!

DISCIPLINE

OH DEAR, WHAT CAN THE MATTER BE
– 2/12/17

BABY CHIOMA, MY treasure, is 10 days old. I have come to spend the weekend with her, as I have done since her birth on November 21st. The previous weekend was fine. She slept with me. I fed her at night. I bathe her in the mornings, and I fed her during the day. I returned for another weekend on December 1st, 2017. Her mother opened the door for me. It looked like she was sleepy. I unpacked and got ready to resume the chores I did the previous weekend.

I received the first shock when her mother said, 'Mummy, please do not carry her. She is getting used to 'hand' - Meaning that Chioma was adapting to being carried rather than adapting to her cot. Meanwhile, Chioma was crying in protest. I thought she was hungry, and I mentioned it.

'No!' her mother said. 'She just wants to be carried. It is not time for her to eat. Her nappy has been changed. She is not going to be carried!' My pleas fell on deaf ears as Chioma's pitiful sobs rang all up the stairs to her mother's bedroom, where she was carried off away from me and my pleading eyes.

I could not bear the continuing cry of the howling newborn infant, and I headed to the mother's bedroom. I saw that her mother sat up on the bed, like one watching an animal in the zoo. The mother had placed her infant in a little bed and continued to stare at her little baby, who was howling her head off.

I immediately carried the baby up and in a quick second, the mother grabbed her baby from my hand and angrily stamped her back on her boat bed, saying, 'No Mummy!! Do not carry her! She wants to be carried. When I carry her, she stops crying, and when I put her down to sleep on her bed, she starts crying!!'

Calmly, I told the first-time mother that the baby was innocent. The baby could not talk. Babies do cry for a reason. 'It is baby Chioma's right to demand the attention she wants.'

'NO MUMMY!!!'

Then I looked at Martha's eyes and saw something - traces of post-natal blues, and so I said, 'Look, you too are crying because the baby is suffering. You are suffering from 'Depression blues'.

'No, I'm not. She is not suffering.'

'She is suffering!' No newborn should be made to cry like this. Is this what she has come to get? Please, my daughter, this is what motherhood is all about. You have to be there for your baby. Please let me carry her.' I hugged my daughter and told her she was doing her best, and quickly took the baby, soothed her to sleep, and gently put her back in her bed. Then I went to my room.

Thirty minutes later, Chioma started screaming. Martha promptly picked her up and began accusing her. I came into the room, looked at the baby and told her mother to burp her. A big burp blew out!

I spoke gently and very quietly to the newly born mother, 'Darling, all babies are innocent. They can't talk. They are newborns adapting to a new world. Every little discomfort is expressed through crying. She is not out to punish you! Remember, she is a gift, a bundle of joy and a blessing. Motherhood is not easy. It is her right to demand that she be fed, carried, etc, when she wants, and you have to comply – PLEASE MY DARLING,' I ended with emphasis. At last, she softened down. She slept with her child for one more hour and surrendered Baby Chioma to me at 5 am. Baby Chioma was glad and cooed,' Thank you, Grandma!'

I fed Chioma, and she dozed off. She woke up at 8:45 to finish the remainder of the 90mls. She slept till 1 pm! She was hungry again and demanded to be fed, but her mother wanted me to bathe the baby first! To keep the newborn mother happy, I sang songs to baby Chioma, which pacified her… As I started to bathe her, Chioma's mother brought me a sponge – big, coarse, but I did not use it. Baby Chioma was surprised to find that she could enjoy a merry bath with music accompaniment. I swaddled her and quickly dressed her up. Her umbilical cord had not dropped...

LAUGHTER

Likes And Dislikes

My husband doesn't like it when I come into the bathroom to use the toilet while he is busy at the sink. This night, I was so pressed. I had just come upstairs to bed and needed the loo. I quickly opened the bathroom door to see my husband at the sink and made for the toilet. Immediately, he bellowed, 'WHAT IS IT? WHAT DO YOU WANT? GET OUT!!'

I quickly sat on the loo. He asked why I didn't go downstairs, and I told him why. 'I am pressed. Suddenly, I burst out laughing and stuff. I could not hold both. He was so angry. He hurriedly did his business and left.

When I finished, I came to the room. I told him I was too pressed to use the downstairs loo. He argued about my doing 'number 2' business [bowel movement], and I laughed. I said that it had been the number 1 business I had intended to do. He persisted that I had deceived him about my actual intention.

I laughed a lot and repeated that I had meant to do a quick pee, but unfortunately, the poo had happened as well! Because I was laughing hard, as I explained, he became all the more angry and said, 'That is why people don't take you seriously.'

I replied, 'People take me seriously. I am laughing because I remembered the story of the kind man who allowed the snake to hide in his belly. The snake saw the sweet liver, kidney and other entrails in the man's belly and … I burst into hard laughter and couldn't complete the story! One good thing had come out of this incident – A good belly laugh!! Laughter is the medicine of the soul. Thank you, Lord Jesus.

PLAY

UNOooo

THIS YEAR, 2019, has passed quickly to April. Most evenings, my beloved and I play UNO cards or Connect 4. As long as he wins, he continues to enjoy playing. I, too, love to win. When I win, the game at hand gets extended until he wins…

TALE

CRYING

IT WAS A Bank Holiday – Monday, May 6, 2019. My son and his wife, who is heavily pregnant, along with our little granddaughter, gave my husband and me a surprise visit at 11:30 am!

I suspended all my computer work to attend to Chioma, who sought my attention instantly.

We all had a jolly time: lunch, gists, updates, naps, and in the midst of it all, Chioma's mum told us a fascinating tale…

She told of how it was just she and Chioma in the house. Chioma was crying off her head, and she did not have the strength to sort out whatever it was that was making her yell. So, she yelled like a baby, and it became a duet between mother and her baby daughter. When Chioma realised her mother was crying, she stopped crying instantly and looked at her mother in askance and wonder – the big question in her pouty baby's face was - WHY ARE YOU TOO CRYING?

TIFF

Sipping Tea – October 28, 2020

'Euuuph...,' my husband takes a sip of his tea. The sound is so irritating that it grinds into my ears.

'Euuuph!!' Another sip. He is having his usual breakfast of Tea, Toast with peanut butter, and frankfurters from half past 10. It is Wednesday. I decide to comment – slowly, softly and quietly, but it is like a barbed dart to his peace and calm.

'Is it so hot?' is all I ask slyly, but it has hit the mark on a spot that turns raw and opens up a can of worms and a cankerous spirit buried deep, which awakens his old nature of fury.

'EUUUUUUPH' - He takes a very loud, rude and deliberate seep on purpose and he is not smiling. He is boiling inside and yet I do not heed the invisible storm.

'Yeah, yeah, we know you are 70!' I say.

I give up in defeat to silence and endure the loud sips. Then he makes his comment – slowly, softly and silently, but it is a barbed dart.

'No wonder some husbands…' I finish up the phrase for him: 'beat up their wives'. He says nothing.

'Not even that,' he says, to indicate something worse than beating up a wife. I throw in more words to help him out to complete the – 'No wonder husbands…'

'Divorce their wives,' I venture. This time, I think that I am correct. Surely. He says no more. His eyes are on the TV, but what he does and says after my following remark shows that 'all that glitters is not gold'.

I say, 'same as women'.

He replies in an outburst, 'CAN YOU NOT GO AWAY FROM HERE? Do you want me to throw this cup of tea at you? Why can't you disappear from here and find something else to do?'

I withdraw. The joke is over. It is too expensive for him. I keep my amusement to myself and say, 'I'm sorry,' and continue with my writing…

ELEPHANT

Mbaise Shylock – September 2021

Salaries at my workplace are paid on the last day of the month. Ever since my husband retired and I had reduced my working hours, I noticed that we had unconsciously adopted a strange and rare policy between us that we never used to do. It is called 'Borrow and Lend'.

He had paid for my laundry and other stuff during the week, which came to £30. I promised to pay back as I normally did, but usually after he reminded me. I had no intention to cheat. I just got forgetful at times. On this occasion, he reminded me about my debt twice and insisted I pay up. I pleaded with him to wait till the end of the month. He refused on the basis that I might default. I reminded him that I had never failed to pay my debts, but more importantly, paying him before my salary came in would put me in the red. I reminded him. Yet, my husband insisted I pay what I owed him. I did, and for a week, I lost money to the bank daily. I decided to borrow the elephant's brain…

CELEBRATION

Birthday? Thanksgiving? Luncheon? What??! July 25, 2021

At the end of today, July 25th, I was tired. I didn't take the time to notice my grandchildren! I was emotionally, physically, and financially exhausted.

My husband wanted a party to mark his 71st birthday, to celebrate Princess's passing her exams, Duchess getting a new job with an amazing salary, and to thank God for granting us another grandson.

It was a rainy day. We all had worked so hard tidying, doing last-minute preparations on shopping and cooking to be ready for the 12.30 party. No one turned up until 2:30 pm. The rain came down heavily at 3 pm. Half of our guests had kept away. There was lots of food, photograph taking, cake cutting, but it was all so informal: No speeches, no singing, but rain! Thank God for the canopy and the abundance of food in our fridge!

About The Author

Olusola Sophia Anyanwu is an educationist, reviewer, encourager, bestselling author and poet. She loves reading books that grab her attention and interest. She says, "I love reading and writing stories that reflect the fascinating lives and relationships between people." Her writings also convey current issues in the world. She also writes Christian fiction and poetry to inspire hope and encouragement. The Holy Spirit of God inspires her. She is a member of the Association of Christian Writers [ACW], Society of Authors, National Poetry Library, Society of Poets, and TRELLIS Poetry Group, UK.

She has 20 books published. As a multi-genre author and poet, she writes on various assorted themes about life. Her works have been featured in the ACW eNews, ACW magazine, ACW blog, and the ACW Bookshop in the

UK and Amazon. Olusola Sophia says, "I want my readers to be carried to lofty heights in the realms of passion, love, faith, adventure, and laughter as they read each of my books. So get a dig in!"

She hopes her writing creates a positive influence on readers, enriches their lives, and gives encouragement and blessings. She is married and blessed with children and grandchildren. She is on Twitter, Facebook, LinkedIn, TikTok, YouTube, Goodreads, Amazon, and Instagram. More about Sophia and her books can be found on her website:

www.olusolasophiaanyanwuauthor.com

Other books by
Olusola Sophia Anyanwu

- Stories for Younger Generations
- Tales for Younger Generations
- Sophia's Fables for Younger Generations
- Stories for Older Generations
- Stories from the Heart
- The New Creatures
- We Can't Breathe
- Turning the Clock Hands Backwards
- The Confession
- The Crown
- Their Journey on Earth to Heaven
- The Robe
- The Captive's Crown

POETRY

- Chameleon and Other Poems
- Sophia's Covid Poetry
- Poetry from the Heart
- Elegies and Dirges
- Echoes of Eco
- From the Womb
- Wings of Faith
- Poetry Matters
- Sweet Slices of Life

www.ingramcontent.com/pod-product-compliance
Lightning Source LLC
Chambersburg PA
CBHW050906180626
46814CB00007B/2923